THE SNEETCHES
AND OTHER STORIES

By

Dr. Seuss

HarperCollins *Children's Books*

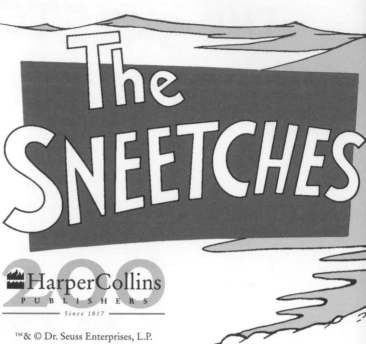

The SNEETCHES

HarperCollins PUBLISHERS
Since 1817

™ & © Dr. Seuss Enterprises, L.P.
All Rights Reserved

A CIP catalogue record for this title is available from the
British Library.

1 3 5 7 9 10 8 6 4 2

ISBN 978-0-00-824004-2

Published by arrangement with
Random House Inc., New York, USA
First published in the UK in 1965
This edition published in the UK 2017 by
HarperCollins *Children's Books,*
a division of HarperCollins*Publishers* Ltd
1 London Bridge Street
London SE1 9GF

www.harpercollins.co.uk

Printed in China

PART OF A SET. NOT FOR INDIVIDUAL RESALE

Now, the Star-Belly Sneetches
Had bellies with stars.
The Plain-Belly Sneetches
Had none upon thars.

Those stars weren't so big. They were really so small
You might think such a thing wouldn't matter at all.

But, because they had stars, all the Star-Belly Sneetches
Would brag, "We're the best kind of Sneetch on the beaches."
With their snoots in the air, they would sniff and they'd snort
"We'll have nothing to do with the Plain-Belly sort!"
And whenever they met some, when they were out walking,
They'd saunter straight past them without even talking.

When the Star-Belly children went out to play ball,
Could a Plain Belly get in the game...? Not at all.
You only could play if your bellies had stars
And the Plain-Belly children had none upon thars.

When the Star-Belly Sneetches had frankfurter roasts
Or picnics or parties or marshmallow toasts,
They never invited the Plain-Belly Sneetches.
They left them out cold, in the dark of the beaches.
They kept them away. Never let them come near.
And that's how they treated them year after year.

Then ONE day, it seems...while the Plain-Belly Sneetches
Were moping and doping alone on the beaches,
Just sitting there wishing their bellies had stars...
A stranger zipped up in the strangest of cars!

"My friends," he announced in a voice clear and keen,
"My name is Sylvester McMonkey McBean.
And I've heard of your troubles. I've heard you're unhappy.
But I can fix that. I'm the Fix-it-Up Chappie.
I've come here to help you. I have what you need.
And my prices are low. And I work at great speed.
And my work is one hundred per cent guaranteed!"

Then, quickly, Sylvester McMonkey McBean
Put together a very peculiar machine.
And he said, "You want stars like a Star-Belly Sneetch...?
My friends, you can have them for three dollars each!"

"Just pay me your money and hop right aboard!"
So they clambered inside. Then the big machine roared
And it klonked. And it bonked. And it jerked. And it berked
And it bopped them about. But the thing really worked!
When the Plain-Belly Sneetches popped out, they had stars!
They actually did. They had stars upon thars!

Then they yelled at the ones who had stars at the start,
"We're exactly like you! You can't tell us apart.
We're all just the same, now, you snooty old smarties!
And now we can go to your frankfurter parties."

"Good grief!" groaned the ones who had stars at the first.
"We're *still* the best Sneetches and they are the worst.
But, now, how in the world will we know," they all frowned,
"If which kind is what, or the other way round?"

Then up came McBean with a very sly wink
And he said, "Things are not quite as bad as you think.
So you don't know who's who. That is perfectly true.
But come with me, friends. Do you know what I'll do?
I'll make you, again, the best Sneetches on beaches
And all it will cost you is ten dollars eaches."

"Belly stars are no longer in style," said McBean.
"What you need is a trip through my Star-*Off* Machine.
This wondrous contraption will take *off* your stars
So you won't look like Sneetches who have them on thars."
And that handy machine
Working very precisely
Removed all the stars from their tummies quite nicely

Then, with snoots in the air, they paraded about
And they opened their beaks and they let out a shout,
"We know who is who! Now there isn't a doubt.
The best kind of Sneetches are Sneetches without!"

Then, of course, those with stars all got frightfully mad.
To be wearing a star now was frightfully bad.
Then, of course, old Sylvester McMonkey McBean
Invited *them* into his Star-Off Machine.

Then, of course from THEN on, as you probably guess,
Things really got into a horrible mess.

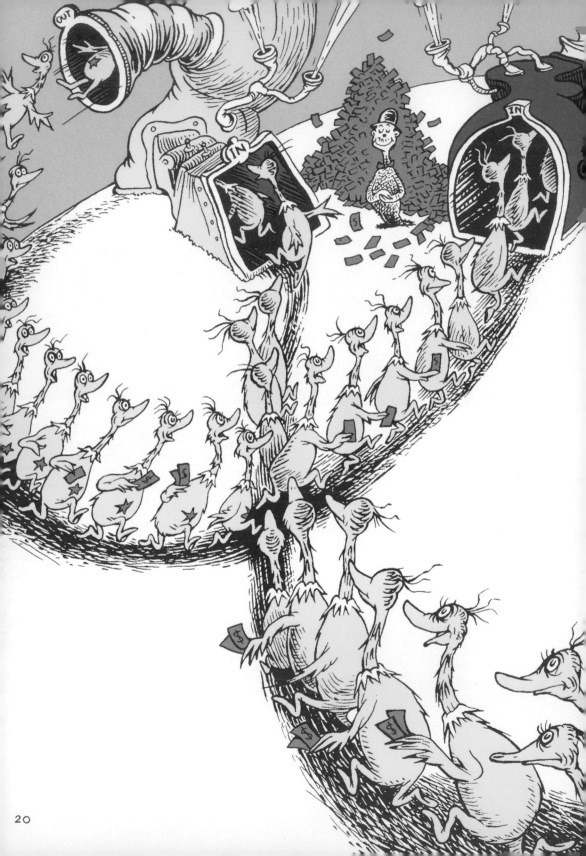

All the rest of that day, on those wild screaming beaches,
The Fix-it-Up Chappie kept fixing up Sneetches.
Off again! On again!
In again! Out again!
Through the machines they raced round and about again,
Changing their stars every minute or two.
They kept paying money. They kept running through
Until neither the Plain nor the Star-Bellies knew
Whether this one was that one . . . or that one was this one
Or which one was what one . . . or what one was who.

Then, when every last cent
Of their money was spent,
The Fix-it-Up Chappie packed up
And he went.

And he laughed as he drove
In his car up the beach,
"They never will learn.
No. You can't teach a Sneetch!"

But McBean was quite wrong. I'm quite happy to say
That the Sneetches got really quite smart on that day,
The day they decided that Sneetches are Sneetches
And no kind of Sneetch is the best on the beaches.
That day, all the Sneetches forgot about stars
And whether they had one, or not, upon thars.

One day, making tracks
In the prairie of Prax,
Came a North-Going Zax
And a South-Going Zax.

And it happened that both of them came to a place
Where they bumped. There they stood.
Foot to foot. Face to face.

"Look here, now!" the North-Going Zax said. "I say!
You are blocking my path. You are right in my way.
I'm a North-Going Zax and I always go north.
Get out of my way, now, and let me go forth!"

"Who's in whose way?" snapped the South-Going Zax.
"I always go south, making south-going tracks.
So you're in MY way! And I ask you to move
And let me go south in my south-going groove."

Then the North-Going Zax puffed his chest up with pride.
"I never," he said, "take a step to one side.
And I'll prove to you that I won't change my ways
If I have to keep standing here fifty-nine days!"

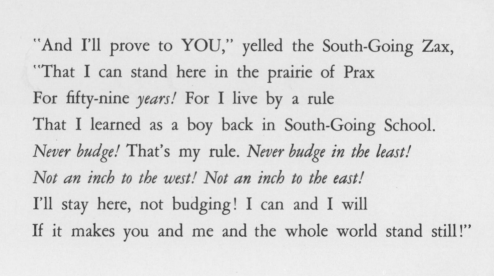

"And I'll prove to YOU," yelled the South-Going Zax,
"That I can stand here in the prairie of Prax
For fifty-nine *years!* For I live by a rule
That I learned as a boy back in South-Going School.
Never budge! That's my rule. *Never budge in the least!*
Not an inch to the west! Not an inch to the east!
I'll stay here, not budging! I can and I will
If it makes you and me and the whole world stand still!"

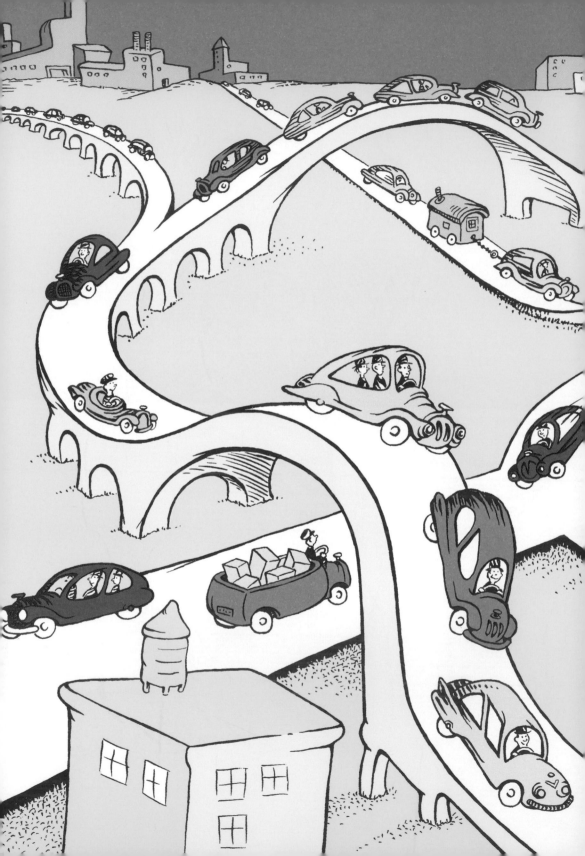

Well . . .

Of course the world *didn't* stand still. The world grew.

In a couple of years, the new highway came through

And they built it right over those two stubborn Zax

And left them there, standing un-budged in their tracks.

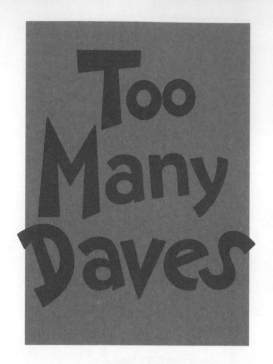

Did I ever tell you that Mrs. McCave
Had twenty-three sons and she named them all Dave?

Well, she did. And that wasn't a smart thing to do.
You see, when she wants one and calls out, "Yoo-Hoo!
Come into the house, Dave!" she doesn't get *one*.
All twenty-three Daves of hers come on the run!

This makes things quite difficult at the McCaves'
As you can imagine, with so many Daves.
And often she wishes that, when they were born,
She had named one of them Bodkin Van Horn
And one of them Hoos-Foos. And one of them Snimm.
And one of them Hot-Shot. And one Sunny Jim.
And one of them Shadrack. And one of them Blinkey.
And one of them Stuffy. And one of them Stinkey.
Another one Putt-Putt. Another one Moon Face.
Another one Marvin O'Gravel Balloon Face.
And one of them Ziggy. And one Soggy Muff.
One Buffalo Bill. And one Biffalo Buff.
And one of them Sneepy. And one Weepy Weed.
And one Paris Garters. And one Harris Tweed.
And one of them Sir Michael Carmichael Zutt
And one of them Oliver Boliver Butt
And one of them Zanzibar Buck-Buck McFate...
But she didn't do it. And now it's too late.

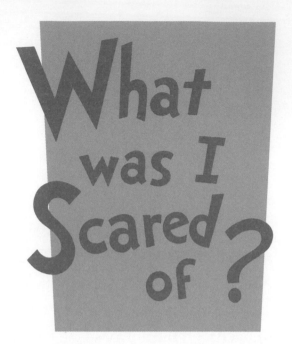

Well...
I was walking in the night
And I saw nothing scary.
For I have never been afraid
Of anything. Not very.

Then I was deep within the woods
When, suddenly, I spied them.
I saw a pair of pale green pants
With nobody inside them!

I wasn't scared. But, yet, I stopped.
What *could* those pants be there for?
What *could* a pair of pants at night
Be standing in the air for?

And then they moved! Those empty pants!
They kind of started jumping.
And then my heart, I must admit,
It kind of started thumping.

So I got out. I got out fast
As fast as I could go, sir.
I wasn't scared. But pants like that
I did not care for. No, sir.

After that, a week went by.
Then one dark night in Grin-itch
(I had to do an errand there
And fetch some Grin-itch spinach)...
Well, I had fetched the spinach.
I was starting back through town
When those pants raced round a corner
And they almost knocked me down!

I lost my Grin-itch spinach
But I didn't even care.
I ran for home! Believe me,
I had really had a scare!

Now, bicycles were never made
For pale green pants to ride 'em,
Especially spooky pale green pants
With nobody inside 'em!

And the NEXT night, I was fishing
For Doubt-trout on Roover River
When those pants came rowing toward me!
Well, I began to shiver.

And by now I was SO frightened
That, I'll tell you, but I hate to...
I screamed and rowed away and lost
My hook and line and bait, too!

I ran and found a Brickel bush.
I hid myself away.
I got brickels in my britches
But I stayed there anyway.

I stayed all night. The next night, too.
I'd be there still, no doubt,
But I had to do an errand
So, the *next* night, I went out.

I had to do an errand,
Had to pick a peck of Snide
In a dark and gloomy Snide-field
That was almost nine miles wide.

I said, "I do not fear those pants
With nobody inside them."
I said, and said, and said those words.
I said them. But I lied them.

Then I reached inside a Snide bush
And the next thing that I knew,
I felt my hand touch someone!
And I'll bet that you know who.

And there I was! Caught in the Snide!
And in that dreadful place
Those spooky, empty pants and I
Were standing face to face!

I yelled for help. I screamed. I shrieked.
I howled. I yowled. I cried,
"Oh, save me from these pale green pants
With nobody inside!"

But then a strange thing happened.
Why, those pants began to cry!
Those pants began to tremble.
They were just as scared as I!

I never heard such whimpering
And I began to see
That I was just as strange to them
As they were strange to me!

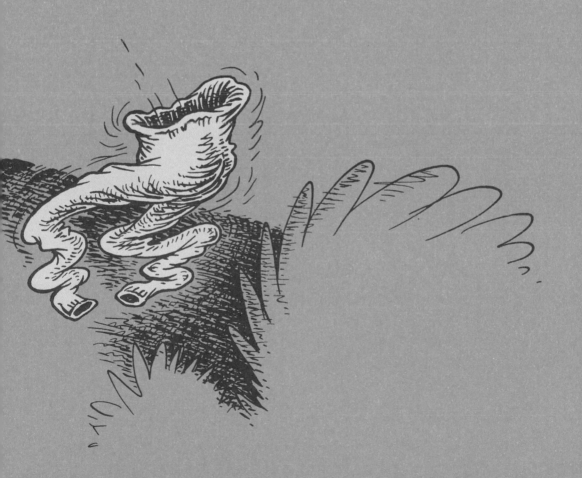

I put my arm around their waist
And sat right down beside them.
I calmed them down.
Poor empty pants
With nobody inside them.

And, now, we meet quite often,
Those empty pants and I,
And we never shake or tremble.
We both smile
And we say
"Hi!"

65